ALL THAT SANG

ALL
THAT
SANG

Lydia Perović

ESPLANADE
Books

THE FICTION SERIES AT VÉHICULE PRESS

Published with the generous assistance of the Canada Council
for the Arts and the Canada Book Fund of the Department
of Canadian Heritage.

Esplanade Books editor: Dimitri Nasrallah
Cover design: David Drummond
Typeset in Minion by Simon Garamond
Printed by Marquis Printing Inc.

LIBRARY AND ARCHIVES CANADA CATALOGUING IN PUBLICATION

Perović, Lydia, 1974-, author
All that sang / Lydia Perović.

Issued in print and electronic formats.
ISBN 978-1-55065-438-7 (paperback). – ISBN 978-1-55065-444-8 (epub)

I. Title.

PS8631.E7345A65 2016   C813'.6   C2015-907347-2

C2015-907348-0

Published by Véhicule Press, Montréal, Québec, Canada
vehiculepress.com

Distributed by LitDistCo in Canada | www.litdistco.ca
Distributed by IPG in the U.S. | www.ipgbook.com

Printed in Canada on FSC certified paper.

For L.E.

To know that one does not write for the other, to know that these things I am going to write will never cause me to be loved by the one I love, to know that writing compensates for nothing, sublimates nothing, that it is precisely *there where you are not*—this is the beginning of writing.

–Roland Barthes, *A Lover's Discourse*

I have battered destructively and in vain upon the mystery of someone else's life and must cease at last.

–Iris Murdoch, *The Sea, The Sea*

1.

Out of the impenetrable fog of sorrow, the shapes of a city will emerge. The colours will divide first out of the blur, the beiges and the whites and the greys of the buildings and pavement, but slowly, so you won't even notice the influx of light. The greys of the clouds will stir once the wind is introduced.

The lines will come into view next, the spikes of the chimneys and slants of the rooftops, the window frames, the chiselled bed for the river, the bridges sloping across. The big tower will pierce its way in, squat and settle, followed by the shorter lines, the antennas, the branches of trees, the eavestroughs, the poles, the gates to courtyards accessible only by code.

Below the street level, the metro will churn to life, tunnelling its way through the city, and by its sheer force set into motion other mechanical and human traffic, cars, buses, scooters, bicycles, strollers and those emergency vehicles that wail better here, more humanely, less unpleasantly, than their Toronto counterparts. As if on a conductor's downbeat, the people will swarm the streets to form the hectic chorales of a weekday morning, moving with purpose this way and that. The noise will surge, disperse, and differentiate, and given that you are in bed, hiding in the penumbra of your rented garret, it will reach you as the ring of the bell from the school on the block, the noise of the TV in the apartment next, the shutting of the doors and the steps in the stairwell.

2.

At exactly 6:05, a visiting construction crew will carelessly dislodge a fire hydrant on rue du Département and the resulting stream of water will flow all the way to the storm drain at the intersection of Marx Dormoy. Two hours later you will have to cross the creek carefully—first your luggage, then you—on your way to the Gare du Nord.

At present moment it is not yet evident that you will leave your bed in time to catch the plane.

3.

Like any other morning, the city insists on re-establishing itself, and the train tracks on both sides of La Chapelle lay themselves down without as much as a cling, one iron bouquet stemming off the Gare du Nord and the other off the Gare de l'Est. Just a little southward, you simply know that the diagonal La Fayette will fall down without ceremony into its usual place, with the very same sidewalk returning, the one you walked the last time you went to meet her. Also there, the same courtyard of the same building where you lingered until the agreed time. The same old woman with a rounded back and a walker will pass through, inevitably, today, on her way out, and the building super will be upset to find an empty cigarette pack in the disused fountain.

Further south, the cake that is the Opéra-Comique will re-layer itself. In years to come, she will again be invited to conduct there.

4.

The eighteenth and the nineteenth arrondissements spread their wings east towards Belleville, cobblestones reset, bicycle paths, canals, social housing buildings like some well integrated spaceships, towards Jean Jaurès Avenue, all the way to Parc de la Villette and the Cité de la musique where you went often, to hear her music.

But also west, towards Montmartre, across Ordener and Barbès and Custine, where once a search for a florist (What flowers should I bring her? What if she doesn't care for flowers?) brought you to the largely black area with a busy and joyful street life.

Further west, Montmartre proper will remount. There are parts of Montmartre so beautiful that they feel unreal, more a theatre or movie set, cosy and perfectly planned. Your own city doesn't have a talent for beautiful display, something in which you take vague pride, because beauty is for sissies, beautiful isn't truthful.

The horseshoe shaped Montmartre street where she lives and all its hôtels particuliers, the Alfred Loos house, the staircases, the mill, the other, neon-outlined mill at the bottom of the hill.

The bench on the other side of her address will remain unoccupied this morning, the one where you sat late one night, hoping to see her as she walked the steps between the taxi and the gate. You had no plan. You hadn't managed to see her after the concert. You missed getting the routine kiss on the cheek, so maybe you'd get a glimpse of her hair.

5.

Across town, among the well off, the Salle Pleyel will reinstall its Art Deco facade. She has frequently conducted there, and the first time you visited was the day when you interviewed her. After the stilted conversation and before the evening concert, you spent the afternoon in Parc Monceau (perfectly replanted to specification this morning). You'll remember the couple, man and woman, standing some metres across from where you were sitting, engaging in what you quickly defined as the most obnoxious public display of affection. They were wrestling at least a quarter of an hour before you decided to leave. They won't be there this morning, but will likely visit the park later this week. It is unsure if they will reoffend.

6.

The city continues to take shape, all the places you went to not to think about her. The Tuileries, where you sat by an empty, yet eager, merry-go-round and thought to yourself, *I am not thinking about her*. Parc Luxembourg, where you observed bocce and removed soft tree leaves from your jacket without thinking about her. The top floor of a university building at the southernmost tip of the city, where during a small theatre performance, two actors, the audience of twelve, you wept, but not because of her (it was a play fashioned from the words said by Marguerite Duras in interviews, some of them rather moving).

Now if you look through the windows of your fifth floor chambre de bonne, you will see a few lighted squares on the building opposite, a figure moving through the kitchen in one of them, another opening the wide double panes onto your street below. If you opened your window now, the wind would rustle the curtains, but you would not be cold. October keeps its douceur here.

It will occur to you that you have in fact completed most of the packing last night, and that the remaining items are all grouped together. There is no strenuous searching activity ahead.

The municipal mender that you came across early yesterday morning at the bicycle station in lower rue Pajol will soon be out on the streets, locating damaged Vélibs and fixing them. *But Madame, that one is broken*, he told you after you'd tried to unhook the one remaining bicycle. *I am finishing this one, it was stolen, but should be all right now, it's back in the fleet, just reattach it from this side, its hinge is a little uneven. Bon courage Madame.*

On your way out you will slip the key into the apartment owner's mailbox, as agreed. It will be near full of advertising flyers.

When you emerge, Marx Dormoy and Boulevard de la Chapelle will be in full motion, it is rush hour quand même, sidewalks densely populated and not easy to navigate, all the stores and kiosks reopened for business, at least two sellers of roast corn that you'll pass, delivery trucks and vans in Little India, the bank where you can withdraw without fees, the windows of the private health clinic where you can see people waiting for their test results, the local pressing, computer and phone hardware stores, but the sound of the wheels on your suitcase against the pavement distinctly cutting through. You are on a straight line, you will reach the train station in good time.

The difficulty returns only once you're there, and have bought your ticket, destination airport Charles de Gaulle. Look for the RER, not the inter-city. There are levels in this station, each marked by different letters and colours. If you are after RER B, it means you are looking for B, not for A or C, no matter how insistently they appear next to the letters RER. It is the red brick section of the station you are after, the one doubling as a shabby shopping mall. You have passed through there many times before, what could be the matter?

There are too many people surrounding you, oblivious to your urgent need to find the letters RER B. You find them finally, go down the escalator with the suitcase next to you, and the train arrives. There is no arrival announcement board. The door opens, you see other people with suitcases on the train, so this must be it. The door closes and suddenly it's unbearably hot. You look up and the blinking light on the digital rendition of the train line is showing Châtelet-Les Halles. You are on the right train but moving in the wrong direction. Soon enough you get off the train at Châtelet-Les Halles, wanting to return. But no sign in sight says RER B, destination Charles de Gaulle. You must focus now. You are hot and confused by the crowd and stunned that she doesn't love you. Why don't those we care for care for us back? It strikes you as a new insight that you are never going to see her again. You must have temporarily forgotten? You ought to move now, and look for the ʙ. Your cross-ocean flight is in two hours. You absolutely cannot afford to stay at Châtelet-Les Halles any longer.

7.

En tout cas, I have no stories to proffer. All I can say reliably is that Paris has always given me grief.

Starting from that very first visit many years ago, when I booked at a cheap hotel promisingly located steps away from the Louvre. That room greeted me with a skeletal lumpy mattress and a shower cabin nurturing generations of grime.

I didn't really care all that much about the Louvre either, truth be told. An outsized department store, more or less. I remember sitting down somewhere in the vast room reserved for the Venus de Milo—sitting down and spotting the statue through the fog of fatigue and saturation. It was a vaguely pleasant feeling. But I've since realized that most museums are best enjoyed via printed photography and text.

No, I was in town on vacation, and to sit in on a class given by Julia Kristeva. She was teaching at that time at one of those numbered sections of the Paris university— vii? xiii? A seminar about Proust and putting pleasure to words and such. So I went to the small seminar room on the scheduled day and time and took notes, and generally passed for one of the graduate students.

The night before, it turned out that the hotel did not have a single blow dryer on the premises, and after I washed my hair in the sink, I left the hair to its own devices.

I have the type of hair that should never be left to its own devices.

So that was that. My hair is always bad for important occasions in Paris. And my skin breaks out. It was like that when I met her, the second time I came to Paris. But I don't want to talk about that yet. Nothing to tell anyway.

I wanted to make it clear that the first time I visited Paris, the Paris innocent of her, not ringing with her presence, I was not entirely adverse to being a tourist doing tourist things. There were lieux de memoire, the ones of the personal reading topography, to honour. There was the pigging out on the cassoulet, and of mornings on the butterthings. But eating alone in Paris is more solitary than eating alone anywhere else. Returning home to the lumpy mattress along the narrow streets that survived the de-medievalization is so heavy in dusk that you realize that dusk probably exists for such returns and those streets—it clinches itself as if to its natural groove and never moves away.

Even now when I'm in Paris, and even when on the bicycle, I come across the unmoving airs of that dusk. You can follow any number of bicycle paths through the city along the boulevards and discover these pockets of stillness, of chilled air, that cannot be disturbed.

The word "Paris", the notion of it, has been filled by the anglophones with so much kitsch nostalgia that it is almost beyond recuperation. That may not be altogether a bad thing, Paris being a permanent misrecognition, now that I look at it closely, something of a dictionary of faux amis that the English and French languages have in common. You can spend a lot of time getting lost and retracing steps along its intricate streets as have I between the delusionary similarities of the two tongues.

Thanks to her, I feel tenderness for Paris now, even France, as nebulous a notion as any other nation. Previously I saw in both only an inward-focused gaze, pre-emptive arrogance. I see them now as fragile, inviting an effusion of protective feeling.

Even if Paris gives me grief.

I am being evasive, obviously. I am not eager to talk about my times in Paris, but that cannot be avoided. If this were a proper story, that's where the story would legitimately start.

But stories are lies by their very build. They eliminate what doesn't fuel them. Why do we need them so? This isn't a story. I can't tell you a story.

I don't know what I'm attempting to tell if I abandon the story, but I know I have that urge. Of telling without storifying. Of writing without re-enchanting. Without tidying. I have the desire to keep the muddle.

Maybe if this were a proper, mutual, happy love story, it would call for a *story* indeed. Maybe two people finding each other warrants a retelling, a founding through a story.

Two people, a man and a woman in particular. But we don't have a man and a woman here.

Maybe if I came from a proper, coherent-appearing, long-historicised country, speaking one language—that is if I came from somewhere other than Canada—I would have also wanted to keep alive the tradition of making stories believable.

Maybe if all of this happened within the same language it would have fit better.

Maybe. Probably.

As it is now, I must speak about what is happening, but I can't give you a story. Plot is a form of self-medication: look, rejoice, there's a glimpse of sense. Fragments will come together to mean something. Let's ignore all what conspires against the narrative.

No.

But off we go, regardless. Paris. Grief. Always. Off we go.

8.

This is what the cameras captured: a woman possessed. There were several cameras positioned inside the apse where the chorus and the orchestra barely all fit in, their monochrome clothing relieved by the colours of the encircling stained glass of the half-cupola. Some cameras only took in details, a section leader with the orchestra, a group of singers, the soloist close-ups; others were reserved for the gros plan. But you don't notice much of this on the first few viewings.

It was a December. Late—maybe even past holidays. A morning spent in bed, viewing the concerts that I had bookmarked earlier on the laptop, reading the things archived in the tabs. I knew of one of the soloists and I knew of her—the few women conductors who achieve visibility easily stand out in images and memory. So that's what such and such has been up to. You salute the recordings. There are more of them, you feel, in the pre-nineteenth century music, and you prefer those earlier periods anyway. It's a side interest that you keep an eye on. But opera is the singers. You come to the concert for the voice, the soloist.

That is one big crowd of musicians: the orchestra, then the chorus, followed by the four soloists and the conductor, fill every inch of the screen to the meek rain of welcoming applause.

Mozart's Mass in C Minor interested me only insofar as its movements in which the solo singers—Laudamus, or Domine—get to impress.

I was standing up already during the Kyrie. It had to be the first time she pierced and slashed with the baton the cloth of sound threatening to engulf her. And how her entire body became electrified. It conducted then released what? Forces of some kind? The pulse gradually asserted itself. An insistent timpani underpins the Kyrie (who knew?) that she punctuated with her head.

There was the body, suited, desexualized, but slight and female, which disturbed the surface and produced sound with its movement. If it grew big and surrounded her, she would fence it off, jump and skip it, sweep it, collect it, dissipate it, halt it, buffer it, withhold it and throw it back. And with the electrified shudder, she would thrust herself into it, penetrate repeatedly.

Kyrie. Gloria. Domine Deus. Qui Tollis. Quoniam. Credo. Sanctus. Benedictus. The flashing white collar of the dress shirt, the black brogue on the resting foot reflecting the lighting.

The cameras are showing too much of everything else, but the director keeps the eye on the conductor during Qui Tollis, the most distressing part of the Mass. It's the wave upon wave of torment, and of observing her whip them and against them and after a while it's difficult to watch.

A deep seriousness within her anchors all the disparate moods of the Mass. There is no hint of even the possibility of distance, ironic or otherwise, of a wink or comedy. This is all there is: I am here, it says, all of me, nothing is pocketed away and sheltered from the emotion, everything is fragile and reverberating, all of me.

Later, when I meet her, I realize that this was the opposite of how she encounters the world: always guarded, maintaining distance, saying only as much as absolutely necessary. Why the reversal? Maybe the first can't be had without the second, maybe there is nothing left after the music. Maybe only the calculating, analytic mind allows for the proportionate and the sedate in conducting, and likewise makes possible the seductively charming communication in the everyday encounters.

For now I am hypnotized, watching her. The credo is practically a dance and the baton moves in fluttery coordination with the bows.

What must it be like to hold her? She looks small, could disappear inside arms. Who are the men who have held her? Because it was probably men. Does she let them? Does she let their hands slide through her hair?

After, I look for other videos of her conducting. She speaks in a low, eloquent, paced, authoritative French with the diphthongal undercurrent from deep in the back of the throat. Rouen, where oue lasts forever and peters out instead of stoppin at the N. Plu. Emu. Et puis. Renouveau. Pâte vocale.

I must meet her, I must write about her, must interview her.

She lives in France and never works on this continent, but the Internet becomes her, the field where I can indulge the gluttony of her images and sounds. It's where I can reliably find her when the need presses. The Internet becomes the archive of her and the body of her.

> *We must be indifferent to each other in order to go on living. It's only when there is a tear in the reality, caused by the occurrences such as falling in love and a sudden overwhelming obsession, that we can see that keeping away from others, not being touched by their existence, is fundamental to life. The one person we love disturbs the happy convivance of indifferent*

strangers. Why doesn't she need my company. Why isn't she curious about me. Why won't she take me.

I am sitting in High Park and observing people who pass by. I may even like them, the young mother with the baby who still can't sit up, the three women on the grass not far from me arguing in Spanish, the couple holding hands, the two men to the left who haven't moved or exchanged a word for quarter of an hour, the too-large families, the old man feeding the ducks when he should know better, the park train driver, the man pushing a stroller, the woman stopping to take a picture of herself with her dog. They're sympa, but I won't be sad because they don't know me, nor I them. I don't need to be part of their lives.

We work and collaborate, then part. We become friends, but can still bear long separations without terrible pain.

Writers and artists whose work changed our lives: we won't feel that we'll die in agony if we remain opaque to them, their personhood, at its most intimate, to us.

It's just that one individual, one dark abyss that drowns the rays of the sunny disposition of amiable indifference, that hints at somewhere parallel and ordinarily out of reach, something that perhaps we shouldn't see.

We must be productive, develop, leave marks, be careerist. Not indulge in self-annihilation. Find pleasures in things other than pain.

Q: Would you say that the aesthetics of your choir have been consistently sombre? The repertoire, Romantic and later, contains a lot of death and despair… and if you listen to nothing but your CDs for days, it can…

The interlocutor is checking her phone.

A: Sorry, I have to see to this. I put it on silent, but now it's telling me something. Just a moment.

Phone handling
Phone handling

Q: [looking around nervously]
A: I wonder what its problem is all of a sudden…

More phone handling

9.

I have only one apartment on Montmartre and I go weekly. I used to go once every two weeks but the owner frequently has visitors during the day now plus has also bought a dog last year and soon after asked Mrs. de Angelis if she could send somebody over every week. The owner works at home a lot, it's understandable. At first I thought Mrs. de Angelis would invite somebody else to split the weeks with me, but no, I continued with both jobs and more work is always good I say.

But I should begin by introducing myself. I am Gabriella, 62 and I work for the agency called De Angelis Cleaning and Concierge Services, voted the Green Business Practices Champion in 2011 by the industry peers. I transcribed that last part from our business card. I should use my own words as we are asked. I am writing this as an exercise in the Improve Your Writing Skills course offered free of charge to the pre-citizenship residents at the community centre near my home in the nineteenth. The instructor asked us to describe something from our work situation that will be interesting to other readers. She just read what I've written so far and had an idea that I try varying how I build the sentences. We can express opposing things in one sentence, she says. Even though [something], I [something]. Even though I did not originally want to come to the class, I did come because a friend convinced me it would be useful and good fun.

Even though the apartment of my Montmartre client is not too large, it is not one of the easiest to clean. (This is how it works, right?) It is very white, the walls and the curtains, and all of the furniture except for the two reclining chairs. And the big car-sized piano in the middle room. There are other smaller musical instruments tucked away in corners. I have never met a woman who conducts music before, but that is what she does. I don't really listen to the serious music—classical music in my mother tongue is also called serious music. In my home country, they would frequently suspend regular TV programming and show concert replays on state TV if a high functionary had suddenly died. A practice that did not help said and similar concerts achieve wild popularity.

We did all sing in choirs growing up. There was much to be told in songs about the newly built country that liberated itself from foreign yokes into a nation of unity and brotherhood.

The white apartment is on the top floor of a building that's already high on the hill, which makes the views worth taking a break for. That is the first thing I go check each time I arrive. Whether everything outside is in order, all the chimneys and rooftops in their right place. We've only spoken once over the last four years, the owner and I, as I usually work best when nobody's at home and come at a time when the clients are likely to be out.

I take the curtains off for a wash every month, but when I don't have to, I use the lint remover rolls, one of my favourite instruments to work with, as far as I can reach. I also try to wash the windows once a month, but if we had bad weather the previous week, maybe more than that, all in consultation with the client via Mrs. De Angelis.

My usual routine is, after I've controlled the curtains and the windows, to start dusting off the objects with electrostatic cloth. A lot of those vases and art objects should not get in contact with water so dry electrostatic is what I would recommend. But you still have to be careful with the work of art far in the corner that has two stick figures hanging in the balance. They are made of fragile stuff—the wire base of their bodies is covered in some sort of paper, that's their skin from what I could gather—and if you touch it, you should touch it lightly. On the mantelpiece, there's a contraption that moves at the slightest pressure on any of its parts. I've given up on trying to dust that one, and that's just fine with the owner. The instruments put away in remote corners I also don't have to bother with. They are wrapped or covered.

What takes up most time are the white surfaces that need to be sprayed and cleaned, plus the mirrors. There is no room for mistakes on those two—the smallest spot is visible. These are the white surfaces: the long coffee table next to the sofa which sometimes has illustrated books on it, the dining room table, the outer frame of the fireplace, the wall-to-wall shelves and closets in the middle room, the bedside tables, and the shelves in the bedroom.

I never vacuum the floors since there are no carpets, but I mop carefully, once wet, once dry. My policy is to change the pail water often: it's not a vast apartment but there's light everywhere and traces of any hasty swiping left to dry will be obvious.

I do the kitchen and bathroom last. The kitchen doesn't seem to be in heavy use, so I don't spend too much time there, but the bathroom is. I would never have guessed it, but it's a girly type of bathroom, with bottles of hair products and skin lotions and sun blocks everywhere. I've never seen this many skin products and ninety percent of my clients are women. I don't mean cosmetics, but bottles of every other kind imaginable, plus she seems to be opposed to throwing anything out—everything is just added to the existing half-used things. I am not allowed to chuck stuff. It's different, the bathroom, from the rest of the house in this way. Too many towels too, some of upscale brands, at least two housecoats hanging on the rack on the door. You can't really move around a lot, but luckily I am not required to tidy up. I sweep the floors (usually end up with a dustball of her auburn hair and some nail clippings) and wash the sink, the tub, and the toilet.

Actually, now I remember. My oldest son's girlfriend used to have a similar bathroom. They used to live together as students, and I would visit and tidy up. Their place always called for a once-over.

I have two grown-up sons back in the Old Country. And their father is still there too. I am a divorced mother of two. I used to be stay-at-home mother until everybody grew up, then I decided it was time to change the situation. It was time, and there were strong reasons.

We are all from the same small Balkan country that emerged after Yugoslavia fell apart. Nobody can tell our small countries apart now. It's good not to be in the international news anymore, however. Can you put however at the end like this?

We don't decorate in all-white in the Old Country—

unless you're a medical clinic. But the more I visit this apartment, the better I understand some of the owner's reasoning. I understand the need for a clean slate. Clearings. Empty surfaces.

Our coordinator asks us to put in how we see ourselves in one year, two years, five years. Where we shall be. Everybody recommends we always strive, and plan, for more. I tell them I've had my share of planning, for members of the family, my own and extended. Now, I am interested in the next day. No: I am interested in the clean lemon smell and having the weather mild enough to be able to open the windows at the end of the cleaning appointment and let everything dry and air. This musician's place is ideal for that because of its view, and because of all the whites.

That's my ambition, that breeze. Yes, it also means task accomplished, something that may lead to more similar work with easily achieved goals, and rent paid in the city I dreamed about and only knew from the films. But it also means simply: that breeze.

Requiem æternam donaeis, Domine, et lux perpetua luceat eis.
Exaudi orationem meam; ad te omnis caro veniet.

Domine, Jesu Christe, Rex gloriæ, libera animas omnium fidelium defunctorum de poenis inferni et de profundo lacu. Libera eas de ore leonis, ne absorbeat eas tartarus, ne cadant in obscurum; sed signifer sanctus Michael repræsentet eas in lucem sanctam,

Quam olim Abrahæ promisisti
Which in Mozart's Requiem I used to hear as the non-sensical "amoriattrae, amorresisti" until I looked it up

Hostias et preces tibi, Domine, laudis offerimus; tu suscipe pro animabus illis, quarum hodie memoriam facimus. Faceas, Domine, de morte transire ad vitam.

Quam olim Abrahæ promisisti et semini ejus.

Benedictus qui venit in nomine Domini.

Agnus Dei, qui tollis peccata mundi, dona eis requiem, sempiternam.

Stabat mater dolorosa
juxta Crucem lacrimosa,

O quam tristis et afflicta
fuit illa benedicta

Eia, Mater, fons amoris
me sentire vim doloris
fac, ut tecum lugeam.

Sancta Mater, istud agas,
crucifixi fige plagas
cordi meo valide.

Fac me tecum pie flere!

Virgo virginum præclara,
mihi iam non sis amara,
fac me tecum plangere.

Quando corpus morietur,
fac, utanimæ donetur
paradisi gloria.

Богородице Дево, радуйся,
Благословенна Ты в женах
и благословен плод чрева Твоего

> For unto us a Child is born
> Unto us a Daughter is given
> And the government shall be upon Her shoulders
> And Her name shall be called: Wonderful!
> Counsellor!
> The Mighty God, the Everlasting Mother!
> The Queen of Peace.

I love those soft pools of melancholy around your eyes. They are like little pillows of uncried tears.

And your chilly blue eyes. Your constellation of freckles. It's ice and the sun, both.

And your lips, always seeming dry and in need of moisture, to be imparted by a kiss perhaps.

The flame of your hair that makes my hands twitch with anticipation.

The long double necklace that your dress shirt collar sometimes opens to reveal, the gleam of it, a touch of obscene disturbing the sombre of the black suit. The crack into a cave, a secret sex, the gold from the depth of the mine.

Q: It's fascinating to me, your love of the nineteenth century and the Romantics in music and other arts. What do you think happened with the notion of love in the Romantic period? Does it get awfully tragic? Do Tristan and Isolde become the model, the all-or-nothing, the ideology of The One? Do we owe it to them?

A: [frowning, blushing] I'm not interested in love. *As a topic? She must have meant as a topic, I'm thinking as I'm transcribing and translating back in Toronto one week later. Yes she **must** have.* What interests me about the nineteenth is their technological advances, love of machines and automatons, their forward-looking attitude, the gravity of their musical feeling—the cheerful choral stuff is rare, and tends to come from folk—the increasing musical complexity, the search for 'melos' as something arising out of a collective of people, not only the elites or musical experts (therefore, further democratization).

10.

It'll be good for our burgeoning arts organization to identify and keep track of our allies in the digital sphere. We should keep them close and grow them. I also think it'll be good for her to meet with her own fan-allies at socials and afters and practise her sociability muscle. We've known each other for a long time before I became her General Manager, and I know that unless there's a particular task ahead of her, her communication style with friendly strangers may come across as unusual—can surprise even. I chalk it up to debilitating shyness, but I've heard less generous interpretations. No matter: the goal is to expand accessibility of classical music through social media and IRL, and that means the accessibility of classical musicians around their profession.

I see the canapés are finally coming out. The catering company we usually hire has shut its door due to a family emergency two days ago, so we had to find somebody quick.

Luckily our next concert is in one week. I am standing in a group of four and the conversation is revolving around the dynamics within the woodwind section. I contribute but, at the moment, I mostly survey the room. Part of my job is forging connections and making sure the already existing connections last. I talk to, therefore, a number of 'food groups' at each of these gatherings, and it's wise to invite a wide cross-section. I see the head of our record label just walked in, so I politely take my leave of the woodwind group and cross the floor to greet him.

We chat for a minute or two until we are joined by the vice-president of a bank that sponsored some of our projects. We know each other well, and I will return to him later for a longer conversation, but I leave the two men as I spot our main government funder taking his coat off. No wife this evening.

But not so fast: the orchestra's youth program officer stops me to introduce me to her latest crop of Youth Welcome Backstage attendees. It's good form to hear about their first impressions. Some of them are high school seniors, others university frosh.

After some minutes, I excuse myself and try to weave my way to the drinks station. While waiting in line, I look around for the Maestra, to see how far she's progressed on her personal chart across the room. She's with the CEO of the venue, an old friend, which is perfect because I should say hello to him—haven't spoken to him since the season opener—and make the ever so diplomatic enquiries about the building site of the new concert hall. I see though that one of the journalists I invited is about to say goodbye to her. It's a real art, the gentle barging-in when the person you want to talk to is with another person. So quickly, she's leaving? I suppose she doesn't know that many people here. Media people are not usually my domain—we have three wonderwomen on staff covering the many sides of media—but we've established something of a mutual Twitter readership, the Canadian and I; whenever she's in town she comes to our concerts, and I invite her to the social part of the evening. As I said, it's good to keep our digital allies interested and appreciated.

I see the Maestra is asking her back for the farewell kiss on the cheek. Why, that's rather sweet. Must remember to put the Canadian on our general announcements press release list. They tailor these distribution lists now very precisely, I'm told, local activities announcements going to the local press etc. We really should look into creating an English-language-only list for international media. Here's a flute of champagne for you, Frau Dirigentin, since our friend here already has a drink. But tell me, I start by asking him, what did you think of the program tonight?

What an eventful period of music history that was, the Napoleonic wars, wouldn't you agree!

11.

When I bicycle up Bathurst, I am also pedaling up Boulevard Sébastopol, direction north on both. That's how the
body recognizes it, the incline is exactly the same degree.
Everything else differs around me, but for a cyclist the
streets resemble one another on the basis of the heart rate.
Sébastopol is wide, Bathurst is wider. Without the trees,
Bathurst, but they will come from Sébastopol. Bathurst
keeps wide and leaves me alone, to my own speed, something
that's impossible for Sébastopol to do.

   Never is the other city more alive in me than in the few
seconds before I finally fall sleep. Thoughts ramble after the
eyes close, and stay nowhere for long, but then they would
come to a stop deep in the eighteenth arrondissement, on
the very specific if arbitrary places along Pajol, very specific
shops, or the overpass on Ordiner, the sidewalks towards
Belleville. As if the camera stopped and the colours became
life-like, the sight of the street filling with presence, with the

right-now—that is the moment when I am about to be lost to sleep. I know I will be gone when there is that zoom-in and sharpening.

It's a matter of time. There is nothing to do about it. I'll wait for time to do its microscopic replacement of the grieving cells. If it is one day, one cell, fine. If it takes a million days.

Sometimes she is the disjointed parts of her body, which I suspect is progress. It's her hands I have difficulty with the most. The memory of the vein that crosses the root of the index finger diagonally, in particular, pulses permanently like an ache. The bulging veins on other women's hands glimpsed anywhere, the rush of circulation breaking through. I've kissed the standout vein, I've mapped its path with my tongue, but not enough times. I've never really kissed her in concentrated prolonged sessions, but I wanted to, and have done so, in my head, countless times. I was always kissing her in my head, in between the instances of living I was permanently kissing, and the kissing was so much more real.

I had to empty all the jars of cinnamon, cocoa and brown sugar. There is no cinnamon, cocoa or brown sugar in the house. I'd tried to find a fitting description for her freckles once and cocoa and cinnamon came to mind, but then I corrected myself: no, they are the brown sugar. This happened once. They wouldn't be smudged or licked off, even though I tried.

I am only halfway from Queen to Bloor on Bathurst. There is fortunately much distance left to cover at this same reassuring pace. A little bit desolate if seen from within a car, but determined, serious, a cyclist is on Bathurst. She earns some respect from the drivers. A figure in an overcoat, she is not in their way. There is a lot of room, she might as well be on Sébastopol. She is pedaling north.

Q: It's remarkable, your activism in favour of increasing the numbers of women conductors in major orchestras. You speak about it often, you have the stats, you yourself even commissioned a survey to obtain the precise numbers for France. The few women in your position tend not to do this kind of activism. They had enough trouble getting where they are and they just don't want to rock the boat.

A: Yes, I know, but nah, I'm not worried for myself. I get plenty of work. It's the issue that's bigger than any individual career that's important here. I know several women who graduated from the conservatory with top grades and are incredibly talented who are not working because the orchestras won't invite them. I am getting tired of this problem, it's beginning to weigh a little too heavily on me. You asked earlier, and I wish I can explain why the women don't get invited. I am resigning myself to the lack of understanding as to why.

Q: *-about to add something-*

A: …and the men, meanwhile, are getting furious. From the man on the street to the decision-makers in classical music, you ask them about this question and they will laugh.

Touched to confusion by this sudden moment of truth-telling and vulnerability. Thinking how I won't be able to use the exact word 'furious' because it will sound too emotional and will alienate the readers—and my editor – who we are trying to win over to the cause.

12. or c 3

00:17 – The resident of the first-floor apartment A2 turned the light on using the ground floor switch closest to the main entrance. He unlocked the mailbox and after browsing the publicity brochures put them all in the grocery bag he was carrying. He scanned the key chain at the inner door entrance and slowly proceeded in. He stopped and at first went to the left, toward the recycling area in the inner court-yard. He stopped again, looked at the brochures again, put them back in the plastic bag. Blackout.

00:22 – The same resident of the first-floor apartment A2 turned the light back on at the recycling room switch, turned right and went up the stairs. He still had the keys in his hand and therefore unlocked the door to his apartment without any further delay. The light stayed on until five minutes expired.

00:30 – The resident of the third-floor apartment C1 left his apartment with dog on the leash and turned the light on at the third-floor switch. The man and the animal descended the stairs at a speedy pace and exited onto the street before the five-minute blackout.

00:47 – The resident of the third-floor apartment C3 entered the building from the street accompanied by another woman, passed through the inner door and turned the light on in the lobby. The two women proceeded up the stairs. At the landing between floors one and two there was a delay. "Not here," said the resident. "The neighbours." An inaudible conversation followed. Blackout.

00:52 – The resident of the third-floor apartment C3 turned the light back on at the landing between floors 1 and 2. The two proceeded to the third floor in silence. A short time later, the door was unlocked and they went in. Then blackout.

01:12 – The resident of the third-floor apartment C1 returned with the dog. He turned the light on in the ground floor lobby, and it stayed on a short time after he let himself back in.

01:21 – The second resident of the third-floor apartment C1 returned. He turned on the light immediately upon entering from the street, opened the mailbox (empty), scanned the key chain at the inner door entrance and got in. He sat down on the fourth stair of the staircase leading up to the first floor. He sat in silence for about a minute. He took a phone out of the coat pocket. When the light went out, he did not immediately turn it back on, the light of the phone being enough for his purpose.

01:30 – Another resident of the third-floor apartment C1 turned the lobby light back on. He ascended the stairs slowly, until at the landing between the second and the third floors he heard the dog from within his residence welcoming his return. He quickened his step so the barking dog behind the door would not have enough time to wake the neighbours up. The light went off when he was inside. The scent of the cologne he was wearing lingered behind him along the staircase.

02:24 – Somebody from C3 left the apartment and sat down on the top stair of the third floor, feet resting on the steps below. It was impossible to tell whether it was the resident or the guest, as the light was never turned on. The individual returned to the apartment a quarter of an hour later. No light came out from the apartment upon the reopening of the door.

05:56 – The resident of the second-floor apartment B3 left the apartment and turned on the second floor light light. He returned to the apartment, pushed out the bicycle, locked the door behind and proceeded down the stairs. He held the bicycle up by the crossbar with both hands and carried it toward the lobby. At the time of his passing through the first floor, the door of the apartment A1 opened to let out the resident woman and the resident child. The neighbours said "good morning", the woman waiting for the man to pass first so as not to be in his way. The woman flicked the switch, which prolonged the timer for another five minutes for both residents. She followed with the child a few steps behind the second-floor resident. She asked the child, "It's all right?" and "It's just an examination, the doctor told us it's quick and you won't feel anything. And then we go for ice cream, good?" The child nodded. The light blacked out one minute after the mother and child left the building.

06:13 – The housekeeper who has the key to apartment B1 let herself in through the main entrance and the lobby door. She turned the light on in the lobby. She proceeded to climb the stairs to the second floor. At the door, she rang the bell. "Right on time," somebody said from the inside and let her in. Lights went out two minutes after.

06:33 – The door on c3 opened to let the guest out. She turned the light on at the switch on the third floor. Between the second and the first floor she passed a deliveryman taking a parcel to b1.

07:04 – The resident of c1 left the apartment with the dog. He did not go out immediately, but knocked on b2 first. There was no answer. He knocked again. No answer. "Come on," the resident of c1 said to the dog, "you'll play with your buddy in the evening. Come along," he said again. He flicked the switch to extend the light before it blacked out.

08:06 – The male resident of a1 and the female and male residents of a3 left their respective abodes almost simultaneously. "Good mornings" were exchanged and a three-voiced conversation about getting to work on time took place. The switch was flicked twice in the course of the conversation, but the three were gone before the second term expired. The woman's high heels were heard distinctly by the residents in a2 and faintly by the residents in b3 and b2.

08:20 – The resident of c3 left her apartment, suitcase on wheels in one hand, dog-carrier bag on the opposite shoulder, a backpack in hand. There was a car waiting. Plenty of time for the light timer, which blacked out well after she was gone, at…

08:25, as the resident of a2 was opening his door. He locked the door behind him, but did not turn the light on. There was enough daylight coming up from the window facing the recycling area in the inner courtyard. He stood there for a while, as if to make up his mind. He turned around, unlocked the door and went back in.

Q: I see you will conduct Orpheus with your new orchestra soon. Who will sing the title role?

A: *-names a countertenor-*

Q: Oh. So it'll be with a guy, not a mezzo.

A: *-seeming to understand exactly why I would say that-*

13.

I will speak out loud the less familiar words as I'm going.

I will *untie*, then *uncoil* your scarf. Round the neck it goes. Once, twice, and it's off. There is always some planning evident in the way your scarves twist and snake, and how their ends meet.

You wear your scarves indoors as well.

A bit like that Canadian pianist who wore scarves and gloves everywhere, but he had the excuse of winter, and numerous phobias.

But what's a man doing in this exchange. Please. Focus here, self.

I am now continuing with the *undressing*.

I am *unbuttoning* your shirt. The whiteness of your dress shirt is blinding to me, so I have to slide down the jacket very carefully. *Tailleur* always sounds better than *jacket*. But I'm not really noticing either; it's the expanse of the white that glows into my eyes and whets them. Also, tears them. As in, wet.

There is so much whiteness for my two hands, which feel small for the task. Small and perhaps dirtied, intruding. This shirt is of the stiffness and sobriety of a nun's habit. Habits are not supposed to be handled this way.

These small buttons call for daintier fingers. *Fumbling* is the word. The little circles resist against the tips of the fingers.

I am *uncovering* the expanse of skin. Every freckle eminently kissable. I see there are freckles on your mouth and over your shoulders.

Straps is a rather curt word. Because they can *glide*, which is a more amenable word, more true to this.

Brassière is more accurate than bra. Well, neither is particularly true, least of all the DIY descriptive term used in French.

No matter, to the *unhooking* now.

There's a blast of high voltage passing through, and I hear only its electric charge and see nothing.

Breasts doesn't do it, not remotely. *Le seine* is weakly better, but not enough either. If the sex is invisible in women, it is really only so in those with slender boyish breasts, who lead with the lower part of their bodies, hands in pockets or behind the back.

My breasts are visible and heavy and phallic. Tedious.

But there is you, now, here, in my field of vision. I could *devour* you. I had forgotten to utter words, so there's a word. If I only could.

I know you're not enjoying this. No, I know you aren't. You would like to undress, rather than be undressed. You prefer your hands on another. This is how you desire. It is in the doing.

You will have your doing, but please let me now.

Le pantalon is better than either trousers or pants. Fact.

The swishy silky sound they make. The crease cutting a sharp angle. The folds and layers, because you are svelte and thin and so are your limbs.

But you are somehow out of my hands and above me now and I can see closely now the little pools of dark and the gentle hives of wrinkles around the unsmiling eyes. (*Wrinkles* is a terribly inadequate, almost comic word. These are pools of softness and shadow.) I can clearly see the freckles against your pale mouth. This -th in *mouth* makes it a little more suitable than *lèvres*.

You are leaving your shirt on and coming over. You are coming above me.

I will be still now.

Your hair may even rain over my face but I will keep my hands down. My mouth may open to take some of it, but I will keep my hands down. I will look and look and take you in that way.

I will be silent. Promise.

14.

Many musicians visit my practice, but she is the only conductor. A number of physical problems are shared among the performing artists, but conductors develop their own. She has complained of chronic back pain, and we've also dealt with Repetitive Stress Injury in the trapezius area of the upper back, as well as the tendon inflammation in the calves. The client used to report spasms in the leg muscles in the middle of the night, the colloquially called charley horse contraction, which lead to awakening, but the incidence has subsided to negligible frequency.

Due to the client's touring and other obligations, she does not come to the practise as often as it would be ideal, but she has managed to reserve the time for chiropractic adjustment on average once every quarter year over the last five years. Busy clients appreciate that the chiropractic sessions do not require disrobing and can be accomplished within the allotted time, without any special preparatory procedures.

With clients in professions with very specific sets of movement, you can predict with a certain degree of precision the recurring physical issues. With the lady conductor, most of our work focuses obviously on the vertebrae and shoulder joints, but often I would add the solar plexus pressure point activation and the simple knee and ankle checkup. Without previously having seen her at work, after the few initial treatments I was able to easily guess the habits and defaults of the client's movement spectrum. In particular I've noticed the recurring effects of what I would describe as the total body tremor, a movement likely caused via the experiencing of an orchestral sound high on decibels and beats. Later on, I managed to connect the effects with what I saw of the client at work, in live concert, and once upon viewing a recording, and indeed it was what I expected. The type of shudder in evidence affects the entire skeleton, and in particular the spinal area and the neck. We have since discussed working on a different distribution of movement, and all too slowly I have noticed some progress. Largely it appears that the client still succumbs to the full body tremor without volition, or rather with a certain abandonment of physical control. Yet exposing the skeletal structure to this kind of electric saw or machine-gun frequency should be phased out.

The skeleton is a remarkable feat of nature, but not everything we do suits it. We should be more aware of the bones, joints, and tendons, and not take them for granted. The job of protection that the skeletal structure performs is extraordinary: within its shelter are the brain, spinal cord, lungs and heart, and the reproductive organs in women. Isn't it a miracle that the softest components of our bodies originate inside the hardest: red cells and platelets inside our bones? Where does one end and the other begin? Bones and blood as one. My wife teases me when I get poetic about my profession in front of our friends, but I can't help it. She says any talk of bones reminds her of her own mortality. She says she would rather not think about the parts of the body that will, as her remnants, outlive her. What can I say? Our early dates weren't exactly easiest in the world.

We have three children now and are one of those un-eventful couples who love each other without drama. I look at my wedding ring as I'm thinking this. I am no stranger to smugness, I am aware of that.

At this moment I am checking the client's vertebrae alignment one by one across the shirt and must discreetly sidestep the vertical bra line. Still, we are well past awkward-ness, the two of us, and chat as two pals at a repair shop would about alignment, preventive measures and the structure under the hood.

In light of her family history and body type, I concluded that she might experience some form of either arthritis or osteoporosis in old age. I've often seen the lean, slight, bony physical types developing either or both, and with some musicians who play instruments I've witnessed various bone deformations in fingers, from diminishment of nails to crookedness in upper fingers and further down in some cases—for example, in string players on large instruments like double bass and cello. But as is the case with many other professions, musicians live with and in fact adopt the minor bodily deformations as a badge of honour. Their instrument is an extra organ, equally cherished as the organs given at birth, therefore some adapting is to be expected.

To feel it in your bones. Something coming too close to the bone. The phrases are not formed by chance. There is wisdom in our bones; the wisdom of the species but also one gained through our own personal history.

The client is a trooper when it comes to pain. I've worked with many people adverse to slightly unpleasant but necessary treatment, and their sessions last longer and involve detailed step-by-step explanation from the practitioner. A couple of times I even received demands for anaesthetics. But generally people are reasonable and under-stand what the treatment looks like. The conductor has a good threshold and is generally cooperative.

Not all of my suggestions take, however. I've recommended yoga before, but I suspect the client's temperament is the opposite to the one required for yoga. The kind of waiting and the passing of time in the posture I suspect would not be her favourite thing, though the facing of the beneficial muscular pain and discomfort head-on and dispersing it through breathing might. She feels that there is never enough time to do everything she wants to, and that an hour of a total halt would confuse her body—if she were to manage to do it. She rather likes that our sessions last no more than 30 minutes.

I will leave the studio and give her a couple of minutes to get back in the gear of the day before she leaves. You are now officially adjusted, Madame, I say, initiating our usual signing-off ritual. I feel super-adjusted, she replies.

Now I must take a quick look at my phone before the next session; our oldest has a loose tooth, and I want to check if a tooth fairy visit needs booking tonight.

15.

Of all of her music, I like most the whisper, the sigh her pressed shirts and suits make as I run my hand across them.

She doesn't need to know this, but sometimes when I wait for her to return, like today, I need the company of her concert clothes lined orderly in the closets. I touch them for their sounds, but also for the feel of them under my fingers; the black vests, coats and blazers are softer to touch than the brusque whites and the sharp edges of the shirts.

There are no skirts or dresses. She hasn't worn a dress since her teens, it puts too many constraints on her, she explains, it makes the body contours visible, and she doesn't like being contemplated in that way. Since we've been seeing each other, I have taken a turn for the feminine. I always felt it required special time and transition, that womanliness, but not when I'm with her. Somehow, the binary jerks its knee and the opposites emerge, a skirt next to the trouser, a décolleté beside the dress shirt. Or maybe I put the dress on for the sole reason of wanting to observe her hand sliding the skirt up my thigh? I have been looking for the signs that will tell me if this difference excites her as much as it does me. She does not share information about her excitements. She does not want to be seen. There, for her, lies freedom. I respect that.

If there is a constant moral striving in her life, it must be this pursuit of ever-greater freedom and autonomy. Perhaps it all started with her teen rebellion (she never goes into great detail) against her own father, an army officer, and a perfectly bourgeois upbringing. Une fille de bonne famille, she was. Her mother often comes to her concerts and the receptions after, and is enormously proud of her daughter, but that is where it ends. They don't exactly visit each other, not even for important occasions. I've been introduced once as a friend, and even then reluctantly. Which is to be expected, given this urge for autonomy. I don't know if her mother knows that she prefers women, but since we see her so rarely, I stopped wondering. It doesn't make any difference whether her mother knows, she is right about that.

So there is the dangerous pleasure of feeling more woman here, in her apartment, than anywhere else, while waiting for her to arrive from the airport. I am in a dress—plain cotton, above knees, half-sleeve, almost a housecoat—and

I've started cooking. I gladly adopt the wifely practises when, all too obliquely, she signals she doesn't mind me to. Flour, water, mashed potatoes, cream, cheese, they work together after initial resistance, salt, sugar, egg whites, coconut, marzipan, I want everything to be white and liquid.

Her apartment barely tolerates the smells of cooking. Had I mastered molecular cooking, our eating occasions would have been more in tune with the white cube, scientific lab atmosphere of her place. One late night when I happened to be here, I craved curry, but I tried imagining the cooking fumes clouding around her floor-to-ceiling score cabinets and her grand and electronic pianos and understood it would be a breach of style. Perhaps the apartment would be more amenable to the smells of baking? Yes, I think so. Something strawberryish, with good grains and nuts. Maybe someday.

I don't sleep over a lot when she is in town, since she likes her mornings to herself. Those times when I stayed, she became very self-conscious, almost shy by what had happened, and suggesting that we breakfast together would have been something of an enforcement, a repeat of an occasion of intimacy. Us being together did not need this unnatural cabaletta—it was enough on its own.

It may not sound like it, but I love her place, though it doesn't like having other people. The long sofa in the living room has a slippery leather cover that's eager to slide you off. The easy chairs are shaped like two pulled-back dentist chairs with no arm rests. The walls of the middle-room with the piano are covered in cabinets and closets. There are mirrors in many places you don't expect to find them, and I pass by hoping they don't maintain my dishevelled and unstyled image for long.

There are inconsistencies, fortunately. The curtains come close to lush and although still strictly white, the length and thickness of their folds evoke a kind of a gigantic Victorian doll's outfit—Emily Dickinson's undergarments —marooned somehow in this apartment at the top of Montmartre.

Her bed is also rather soft and everything in her bedroom too—throws, blankets and extra cushions orderly awaiting. She prefers them like that. My dream is to orchestrate a big mess in her bedroom—the bed unmade, tongues of the coverlets hanging off any which way, pillows on the floor—and just maintain it for a while. To what purpose, I don't know. To touch her by irritation? Too easy. Perhaps to leave the very temporary graffiti on this enviable, self-sufficient fortress she's maintained for herself.

The anarchy of Paris as a view though, that's probably what stands out in the white cube. On the side of the middle room, the branches often bustle in the wind, birds flap past, but the living room is wide open to the neighbouring seventeenth and the eighth arrondisements, starting with the unglamourous backyards and the entrails of the apartment buildings, decaying chimneys, rusting iron balconies with greying potted plants, further to the more upscale Paris trademark buildings and the Eiffel Tower in the distance, not disregarding the office towers of the well-off western suburb discernible in the mists across the Périphérique.

16.

Has it been four years since I first saw this apartment, when I failed to notice its details and peculiarities and consequently couldn't describe them in my interview? When she suggested I talk to her at her home office, where she often invited journalists, I thought I would have a good look at her artwork and have a paragraph worth of descriptions of the conductor in her natural habitat. In the event, I was too stressed to notice anything more than the toy cars—which turned out to be an artwork too, not a collection—and the consistently white atmosphere around me. She didn't smile when she opened the door, and immediately disappeared in the kitchen. It took several more encounters for me to realize that her internal film often sometimes runs independently of whatever external ones she may find herself sharing with others. It is a question of the inner screen, I believe, never ceasing the play of its shadows. She sometimes appears inward-looking even in situations of intimacy. Before she got to know me and trust me, I wasn't a stranger to her unease in social situations. The way out of a conversation for her is sometimes walking out of the conversation, leaving before the sentence is over, hers or the other person's. Perhaps the pressure of inadequate words becomes too suffocating. Perhaps language anchors her like pinning a butterfly, too precisely for a creature made of air and flight. As we got to know each other better, there was less of the rapid flight, but not many more words. She would stay in my arms, though. Ça, c'est pas rien.

I mean, she was put in boarding school age 11, where she shared the dorm rooms with dozens of other girls. Before that, she was one of several siblings in a large family. She was visible to all growing up, and later in school she was constantly under the watchful eyes of dozens of girls and teachers. I don't want to appear to be prying so I don't ask too much about this, but it's easy to draw conclusions. Music was a door to elsewhere, un jardin secret.

Words are not her favourite medium, did I mention?

For the longest time I was sure she didn't like me or even notice me, yet I kept travelling to see her, for concerts and social occasions around concerts. We would talk briefly, then she would be required elsewhere in the room, and each time I'd make a point—a ceremony, a ritual—of saying goodbye before I left. On one such occasion, she stopped me from going when I was already coming down the stairs and asked me to return. "Viens, viens, viens," she demanded, and expected to be kissed on the cheek. After a few words were said, she allowed, Okay now you can go.

17.

Flour, milk, water, whites. Everything is coming together, the dough and the liquid. I work with my hands. The texture is becoming thicker. It has to have the right consistency and temperature.

After that, she still remained elusive.

One time when I was in Paris, listening to the radio, an interview with her came up. Near the end she shared that she was eager to go to the second Bruckner concert in a row conducted by her own favourite conductor at the Salle Pleyel that very night, in fact, after she finished the interview at France Musique. It was too late for me to get the ticket, but I looked up the concert online and figured I could make it to Salle Pleyel for the final exeunt of the audience. I dressed in formal camouflage and the taxi took me through Boulevard de la Chapelle and Boulevard des Batignolles, to the part of Paris that was silent at night, de Courcelle, darker and more silent still, to Avenue Hoche and rue de Faubourg Saint-Honoré all deserted by humans and even cars, active life staying behind closed windows and doors of apartments. What was I going to do? I had no clear intention. Only the hope that I would see her, whether alone or with somebody, walking out onto the street, perhaps lingering at the entrance to finish the conversation before taking the final leave. It transpired that the online ending time had been inaccurate and I arrived after everybody had already left the Pleyel. There were cafes on Faubourg filled with people, but everything was set to low volume. I was so struck by the silent Paris that I stopped and listened. I looked for signs of her inside the quiet restaurants, and on the deserted sidewalks around the sleeping parked cars.

She remains elusive even now. But everybody has to put up with something. There is no such thing as a perfect relationship. If it's not one thing, it's another.

It took several more visits crowded with other people before we met alone. I had prepared a long speech. Have you ever desired anybody so much that your every waking moment was occupied by the thought of that person? She interrupted me by taking my hand. I took hers in turn and kissed it.

We really have nothing in common, I imagine myself saying to the camera in a hypothetical documentary film about her life. This one is different from the others as it's the first one in which she talks about her personal life. It's almost a comedy routine between the two of us in this sequence. *She speaks French, I speak English. She likes Schumann and Brahms, I like Monteverdi and Bach.* Food is among her pleasures, she says of me. *Whereas, she doesn't eat.* I speak German, she speaks Italian. *I have the build of a Slav peasantwoman. Y'know, equipped to plough the fields and raise healthy cannon fodder. Whereas she is the slender, freckly, Isabelle Huppert type meant to occupy salons… and concert halls.* I like wine, she likes gin. *I can't even read music. She is music, damn her.* She takes words seriously. *She uses them all too lightly, like an inflated currency that has never had its gold standard.* I get around on a scooter or car, she pedals around. *She hangs out with rich people.* She automatically presumes everybody who's not struggling to survive is somehow bad—and success is suspect. *Yeah I guess it's fair to say she's more to the right.* You are extravagantly left from where I stand. *She's into the Romantic era and the nineteenth. Like, Heathcliff is her brother in turmoil. Victorian Gothic is the normal.* Oh so the seicento and the settecento are, like, closer to our era's sensibilities somehow? *I can't believe you worship Schumann. Go listen to some Frauenliebe und -leben.* And you those silly fiorituras in Benedetto Ferrari. *How could we have ever become close?* We love each other, I suppose. *Oh right, there's that.*

We don't really talk in that way, but in this documentary we would.

I moved to Paris so I could stop travelling to see her and share a city with her. Why not, she said when I suggested it. I can write from anywhere, I added in case she wondered whether it was prudent for me to leave for the other side of the Atlantic. We can try, without any definite conclusions, and see how it goes. Seeing each other more, I mean. She nodded.

She didn't object to the idea. She didn't say, Is that necessary? She looked pleased. The past months have taught us that I had foresight—there were times when she needed me. When she did, I was there, and nobody would have been had I not moved close to her.

I did not know she preferred women until the moment she let me kiss her hand. There is a documentary, one of the actual ones made about her, in which she is shown being treated by a chiropractor. We observe a pair of young male hands and arms, tanned and hairy against her white shirt, adjusting her bones, pressing her solar plexus, stretching her neck, counting the vertebrae. A gay woman would be aware of the connotations of such imagery and would not have agreed to be recorded, I was certain.

I teach English a lot now here in France.

As for her, she sounds more feminine in English—in

French she is a deep nasal alto; her voice goes higher and a little more insecure in English, as if some ladders have fallen down and there she is, on a trapeze. I suggested her English needs butching up. She doesn't disagree.

Not having a common language in which we are both fluent can be advantageous—the bodies have to find their way into knowledge without the words. But still I envy the natural ease with which other French speakers slip in and out of conversation with her. There is a sort of shared non-verbal familiarity to fall back on.

Well, I have so much to tell her. In English, because I need all the eloquence I can summon.

Cue the doorbell. The dog. She is back she is back she is finally back.

18.

How was Vienna? Tell me all.

She hugs me and brushes her mouth against my cheek, then is preoccupied with putting away the coat and the luggage. My hands around her manage to feel her lean build firm and tense for a moment before we separate. Are you tired, are you hungry, there is food. The dog is meandering among our legs, and she says she is worried for it, it suffered stomach aches on the trip, and her words about arranging a vet visit trail off as she follows it to the other room.

From 1 to 10 on the Absence Scale, I think she is a 6 to 7 now. Nothing I can't handle.

Once at the table, she's noticing the food. The gnocchi in her plate are melting into their own gooey puddle. She moves them around, picks up one with a fork, but the rest won't let it go, the cheese in the food binding everything with strings. There is an almost sloshing sound to it. Also on the table, an open pot of creamy clam chowder, and a cold pudding with white coconut sauce. Perhaps belabouring the point, I also filled the champagne flutes with almond milk. She considers one after another, and realizes just as she asks Why is everything… Oh I see. She lowers her gaze, would I say almost timidly? I would.

Why is everything the colour and consistency of female arousal, she doesn't ask but it's understood. There has been some shyness lately on her part, something of the return of the insidious pudique, the term I can't properly translate into English since modest, puritan and chaste don't come close. Have you met someone else, countless cliché house-wives have asked their husbands in countless cliché recits after their sexual encounters wane, and I'll spare everybody that scene. Besides, it can't be that.

Yes, the food is like this because I've missed you, obviously. This is how I feel physically while you're away. Before we got together I used to spend an inordinate amount of time on the internet looking at her conduct in concerts and listening to her recordings, but after we got together that hasn't changed. Her Internet self keeps me company every day, probably more than her physical self, probably a little too much, but that is my problem. She is available enough—it's just that on some days that enough is less than enough for me so I seek her digital images and sounds. What has changed is that those images of her are now imbued with an irrepressible life; I know now how her percussive or ornamental or beat-keeping gestures connect with how she is intimately, and this has on some viewings driven me insane. Now I find myself flooded in milky waters, high-strung with excitement, as much from watching a recording as I can get at a live performance.

I try to tell her some of this as I sit down on her lap and wrap my arms around her neck like a schoolgirl. Now she really notices my bare feet that I nestled on top of her laceups and strokes my thighs doucement under the skirt as I had hoped she would all day. She tells me to be good and let her eat just as I start to play with her hair.

Well okay. Yes. I return to my chair. Bits of paper rustle in my pockets—the notes I've taken for things that I need to say. Next week we have the nights only, with her rehearsals starting anew tomorrow, and the nights are not the best time for relationship talks. We go out to concerts or the theatre, or exceptionally we spend a languorous silent evening of lying in bed next to each other. (Absence Scale reading about 3, but feeling her weight in my arms or following the trail of her freckles from neck to calves makes up for any lack of conversation.)

She tells me about the tour—Vienna, Graz, Venice, Munich, Berlin—in basic strokes. *Were there any sopranos or mezzos that you desired*, I might ask in the future, when our relationship is deeper and we can air out and even make fun of our fears, and even perhaps have a system of a loving non-monogamy established. Gay men do it all the time, it can be done. Were the soloists behaving, I actually ask. And in the mix of professional and personal information given in response, I parse for things to keep. It's hermeneutical hysteria, a friend told me on the phone, after I described the early days of my obsessive love for her. You look for signs everywhere and infer solid truths from the contingent occurrences, he said. He recently asked if, now that we're finally together and safe, I've stopped doing it. Nobody is every together and safe, I informed him.

I tell her I watched the multi-cam broadcast of the Berlin concert online and that if you linger on the conductor camera for some time, it becomes obvious that she knows the score inside out, every bar, every entry, and you can see her anticipate it all a split second before with her gestures. You in fact not only know the score by heart, your body knows it in its core—in the core of the body a music score, ha—and serve as its conductor, it's really impressive. She is amused, then becomes serious and looks at me directly, as if enjoying the thought, but briefly, as if immediately remembering that I would be biased, I would say that.

We find ourselves in silence. Or not quite; from the other room there's the sound of the radio and the pings of the arriving email, and here the patter of little paws, but also her own legs getting restless under the table.

Can I talk to you about something, I say and regret how I phrased it. It sounds like I'm about to plead. Or like a domestic situation. If there's one thing I avoid, it's the creation of domestic situations, she had told me once. You're right! Those are dreadful. But then I thought, wait. C'est quoi une scène domestique? Oh you know what I mean.

Yes, perhaps we should talk, she said. Which is not what I expected she would say. She usually says, we're good, there isn't much to talk about, why fix what's not broken, etcetera.

19.

You know the Handel opera *Alcina*, was how I was going to start. A sorceress enchants people she loves and keeps them on her island? Well, there's this character in it, Ruggiero, sung by a mezzo, Alcina's favourite, that mainly just mopes around the island to great music, wondering why she in the state she's in, paralyzed yet happily high, not at all herself but somehow taking pleasure in the fact? She was going to nod sympathetically here. Ruggiero is the badly written character of the opera. She is a roaming shadow and can only think one thought: Alcina.

That's how I feel. I've been the badly written character in my own life ever since I've met you—seen you, actually, really taken you in, probably since Mozart's C minor mass. I don't want this to stop, I'm saying the opposite: let me come closer. I am dying to go further into your life, not just as an enchanted fool roaming the outskirts. Let me travel with you sometimes. Let me kiss you in public. Let's go to things together; not as friends but together. Show me when you need me, don't make me guess. Expect me when you need me. Every cell of me needs you, but that doesn't matter, I don't have any demands. Well, except perhaps at this very moment if we can make love on this table right here because I haven't had a proper taste of you in two agonizing weeks.

Before I managed to say anything, she got up from the table and began changing from her travel clothes and said, Go on. I'm listening.

What am I to you, is what I said, the worst wife-like utterance imaginable, and I could see that she slightly cringed though she was turned sideways, unbuttoning her shirt. That's not what I meant to say. I meant to say, I said, what harm is there in travelling together? I miss you too much when you are away, and you are often away. I don't have to stay the entire time, I can come for a few days.

The endless unbuttoning. She seems to be pondering this.

And all right, yes, I guess I am wondering what it is that we are doing. Together. And if we are.

She held on to the closet door to release first one leg then the other from the trousers.

I never know if upon any of your returns you will still like me or not.

She sighed in a certain spirit of commiseration, and after putting on her at-home clothes she joined me on the sofa.

She stroked my knee gently for a while, then finally said:

And there I was, in the airport taxi today, thinking all the way to here how to suggest that we should perhaps slow down a little, not take it so seriously so quickly. No, no, darling girl, you mustn't now. We can't talk if there are tears happening.

Sorry yes, this is embarrassing. I'm good.

She told me other things, perfectly reasonable things that I really should have guessed already. That her life was full and she was content with it as it was, there is simply no room for any radical rearrangements, that ideally it must go on in the exact way it is going now. That she likes seeing me, but that it pains her to see me unsatisfied, lonely, in our admittedly very loose association. That—and she said this very gently, not a trace of cruelty—she probably should have discouraged me from moving to Paris, and giving what we have a narrative that it can't have. And that I know well, if I know her at all, that she prefers to flee other people's narrations, that the telling, the analyzing, the naming tires her, that really she can't be in anybody's story.

No, there wasn't anybody else, she said and didn't laugh it off when I asked. After I expressed disbelief, she shrugged her shoulders almost sadly, and begged me to try to understand. There was nobody else. She loved her life as it was, she loved getting home exhausted from a day of grappling with music, of being windblown by it in every imaginable way—as a weathervane at the crossing of the conflicting streams of sound.

She brought me tissue and tried to make me feel better by making me remember the silly moments we had together. I was embarrassed by her kindness and couldn't look at her, but focused on ripping the edges of the used handkerchief in my hands. When I put it away in my pocket, it brushed against the notes still there. I remembered what was on them.

Alcina's-Ruggiero: mostly mopes around the island.
Badly written character because obvs. nothing else to do.
That was me / in my own life.
Travel. Kiss. Attend together. Need, specific when.
How about this table, now?

I can't, this is unbearable. I must do it differently.

20.

The bell rings: she is finally here. How was Vienna? Tell me all.

She draws me close and kisses me with conviction, and when I come up for breath I tell her how I awfully *kiss* terribly *kiss* schoolgirlishly *kiss* desperately *kiss* I have missed her these two weeks. The yelping of this dog of yours describes how I felt very accurately.

She's been ill, the little beast. I'll have to take her to the vet, the cutest pest, and my rehearsals start tomorrow. Yet another thing to do. What between collecting my clothes from the pressing, the dog's moods, fending off the mother's invitations to lunch, and these breasts of yours, how am I supposed to stay focused these days? I go to work to relax, I tell you.

I'm sure I can be bribed in *some* way to consider taking the dog to the vet for you tomorrow, I say.

Oh? Oh. I'll put my mind to it, then. I'm sure I can come up with something.

But first we dance around the apartment to no music, and I kiss her neck and take her necklace in my mouth— sorry my dear, my clothes smell of planes and trains, she offers, but all I care about is the area on her chest where the freckles converge into a dense hive. I toss away her blazer.

Well, how was it?

Where to begin? The soloists. The tenor was a drama queen. The bass was a prick. The soprano and the mezzo hated each other, but became friends near the end, after they found a common enemy. (You, I hope? Qui d'autre, chouchoute.) "I've never sung this piece that way before" raised its head a few times. The orchestras? Three out of five—seduced. One civil, but much too sedate. The remaining one chiefly civil, often illegible. The first violin in one of these, I am trying to forget which one, kept wanting to chat with me about Beethoven, he did his doctorate on the symphonies you see and may have some useful things to share about the historical context, but the gods had mercy and got him drunk rather quickly at the reception after the concert. At another after, an Italian businessman suggested I might get their corporate sponsorship if I met him for drinks later. (Ooh, sexay. You can have my corporate sponsorship of your veterinary duties if and only if you let me top you over the next 24 hours.)

And so we talk nonsense. She looks at the food and states that I appear to have managed to make dinner out of female cum and that she wants to try it now in all the recipes. She improvises a few variations on that joke—has it been the secret ingredient of your cooking all along, and the like. She asks me what I've been doing, whether I've been behaving in her absence, what I've been writing about. She won't let me go for a long time; her hands, what feels like six of them, are reshaping and sculpting my body into existence, make my skin trill in the ache of rebirth. Have I watched the concert online, she wants to know, were my senses excited, did the music excite, did she excite me as other times (I can only nod to along to each question), did I especially feel it here, or perhaps here.

It looked as if we were about to fuck on the dining table, my head nestled close to the steaming pots and the clinging cutlery, when she stopped, kissed my knee and said, We have to talk, love.

We sat on the sofa and she chose that moment to tell me the reason for her increasingly frequent travel to Vienna on work-unrelated matters. The woman she had loved when they were both students of music—her first great love, she added—came to one of her concerts earlier this year, after fifteen years of mutual avoidance. They talked, reminisced about good times and bad, and agreed how wonderful it was to be over one another, that they could now resume their friendship as two rational individuals. They did start meeting whenever one was in Paris or the other one in Vienna, but strangely, she says, by stating that we can finally be friends we called into existence the opposite. How do you mean, I asked, getting to my feet, I don't understand. Well it doesn't matter how it happened—it happened, we remembered what we'd once been to each other and... anyway. I need her back in my life in some capacity.

And before you say anything, please listen to me. This doesn't need to change anything between us. You will say that I'm the only thing you desire, but that can't be true. You must honour your other desires, futures, languages, never *ever* neglect them because of me, think of me as the ornamentation, or the bass line, not the lead melody. And there is no need for any of us to be unhappy. Let's be good to each other.

What I managed to say was that she was breaking my heart. And that I didn't know what to think and what to feel. But that I didn't like this. Who was this person?

You can meet her, she said. You will meet her. You must meet her. I'll have this visiting conductor contract in Austria next year, I will be able to meet with her there, but when I'm back in Paris, I'll be all yours. I hope you'll be mine too. I want you to stay. I need you as much as I need her.

On some holidays, we might invite her to Paris. But that will be exceptional, and only if you are fine with it.

She started taking off her clothes and preparing for a bath, all the while talking very sweetly to me, arguing very soundly about our future life, about the fact that not much will change, and that she owed me nothing but full honesty.

I hear the water running for her hot bath and go to the bedroom to hide under the duvet. This is so unfair, I yell. I can't even hate you now, you're dumping me so brilliantly.

Oh but is that word necessary, I hear her respond. Come and join me in the bathtub.

Is she singing in the bath? Oh my god, she is singing. I shut the bedroom door and put on the first dramatic thing I can find, the Mozart Requiem, but the one with modern instruments, the Karajan one, the one she loves to hate. The loudest possible Kyrie is rising and twirling around the room (*very funny!* she shouts pretend-offended from the bath), but by the time Dies Irae starts, I know I must put my shoes on, collect the few objects I can't bear to leave behind, and be gone before she comes out.

21.

France has one of the best railway systems in the European Union. The urban, suburban and inter-city trains operate according to the publicly available schedules ninety-eight percent of the time. Delays, be they major or minor, are rare. The internal signalization is reliable, communication with the public is reliable, and the only thing occasionally perhaps found wanting, if we want to insist on it, is the appearance of a select—low!—number of older stations on the RER grid.

But no station, including those, is ever devoid of friendly-appearing people. The stops may be hectic but never hostile, and there are always a few congenial people on the platform that look like they'd be a kindly source of information on directions. It's a statistical inevitability.

Indeed not far from you is one such person, and after you manage to scramble a question for him, he directs you to the right escalator for the right walkway to the platform where the RER B for Charles de Gaulle will reliably stop within the next five minutes.

You even find a seat on that train.

22.

Because time also is a story, a montage, something that we craft, something through which we disperse what we can't approach head-on at once, it is untrue. Time is *not*, not really, and everything that emerges goes on as has previously gone on, except not within our sight or knowledge.

Once you have called me to come back up the small flight of stairs to kiss me goodbye, it cannot be undone. It cannot not exist. You are at the same after-concert reception, with the same people as on that night, forever spotting me leave, forever not letting me go before you're done, forever saying "Viens, viens, viens" to me in that very same way, and I am always and forever turning back and coming to you and settling my cheek next to yours for a kiss.

THANKS

To my editor Dimitri Nasrallah, for believing in this book even before I did, and unstintingly. For understanding it, down to its most bizarre corner. For reassuring me that I am not a madwoman. (I suspect he's wrong on that one.) For the freedom.

To Simon Dardick for his work on the making of this book, and for his trust. His sense of humour. For challenging me on Verdi's *Requiem*. For loving the mezzo timbre.

To Julie Joosten, who was the very first and thoughtful reader of the manuscript. For her poetic sense. Her asceticism with words. Erudition.

For the influence through their work, Keith Ridgway and Siri Hustvedt, who know how to approach and write the void and whose books helped me dare approach the void I needed to look at.

To the Dashing Man, who probably understood everything, the said and the unsaid.

To the musician who inspired (that old-fashioned word) this book. And may she forgive me for putting her in the position of the muse. The muse is not inherently passive. She fathers, engenders: the rest of us just carry out.

ESPLANADE
Books

THE FICTION SERIES AT VÉHICULE PRESS

Véhicule Press